'I, a demon, bear witness that there are no more demons left. Why demons, when man himself is a demon? Why persuade to evil someone who is already convinced? I am the last of the persuaders'

ISAAC BASHEVIS SINGER
Born 21 November 1904, Leoncin, near Warsaw,
Russian Empire
Died 24 July 1991, Surfside, Florida

'The Last Demon' and 'Yentl the Yeshiva Boy' first
published in book form in *Short Friday and Other Stories*
(1964). 'The Cafeteria' first published in book form in
A Friend of Kafka and Other Stories (1970).

ISAAC BASHEVIS SINGER

The Last Demon

PENGUIN BOOKS

PENGUIN CLASSICS

Published by the Penguin Group
Penguin Books Ltd, 80 Strand, London WC2R 0RL, England
Penguin Group (USA), Inc., 375 Hudson Street, New York, New York 10014, USA
Penguin Group (Canada), 90 Eglinton Avenue East, Suite 700, Toronto, Ontario,
Canada M4P 2Y3 (a division of Pearson Penguin Canada Inc.)
Penguin Ireland, 25 St Stephen's Green, Dublin 2, Ireland (a division of Penguin Books Ltd)
Penguin Group (Australia), 250 Camberwell Road, Camberwell, Victoria 3124, Australia
(a division of Pearson Australia Group Pty Ltd)
Penguin Books India Pvt Ltd, 11 Community Centre, Panchsheel Park,
New Delhi – 110 017, India
Penguin Group (NZ), 67 Apollo Drive, Rosedale, North Shore 0632, New Zealand
(a division of Pearson New Zealand Ltd)
Penguin Books (South Africa) (Pty) Ltd, 24 Sturdee Avenue, Rosebank, Johannesburg 2196,
South Africa

Penguin Books Ltd, Registered Offices: 80 Strand, London WC2R 0RL, England

www.penguin.com

Selected from *The Collected Stories*, published by Farrar, Straus and Giroux 1996
This edition published in Penguin Classics 2011
1

'The Last Demon' translated by Martha Glicklich and Cecil Hemley
'Yentl the Yeshiva Boy' translated by Marion Magid and Elizabeth Pollet
'The Cafeteria' translated by the author and Dorothea Straus

Copyright renewed © Isaac Bashevis Singer, 1981, 1982

Typeset by Jouve (UK), Milton Keynes
Printed in England by Clays Ltd, St Ives plc

ISBN: 978-0-141-19623-7

www.greenpenguin.co.uk

Penguin Books is committed to a sustainable future
for our business, our readers and our planet.
The book in your hands is made from paper
certified by the Forest Stewardship Council.

Contents

The Last Demon

I

I, a demon, bear witness that there are no more demons left. Why demons, when man himself is a demon? Why persuade to evil someone who is already convinced? I am the last of the persuaders. I board in an attic in Tishevitz and draw my sustenance from a Yiddish storybook, a leftover from the days before the great catastrophe. The stories in the book are pablum and duck milk, but the Hebrew letters have a weight of their own. I don't have to tell you that I am a Jew. What else, a Gentile? I've heard that there are Gentile demons, but I don't know any, nor do I wish to know them. Jacob and Esau don't become in-laws.

I came here from Lublin. Tishevitz is a godforsaken village; Adam didn't even stop to pee there. It's so small that a wagon goes through town and the horse is in the marketplace just as the rear wheels reach the toll gate.

There is mud in Tishevitz from Sukkoth until Tishe b'Av. The goats of the town don't need to lift their beards to chew at the thatched roofs of the cottages. Hens roost in the middle of the streets. Birds build nests in the women's bonnets. In the tailor's synagogue a billy goat is the tenth in the quorum.

Don't ask me how I managed to get to this smallest letter in the smallest of all prayer books. But when Asmodeus bids you go, you go. After Lublin the road is familiar as far as Zamosc. From there on you are on your own. I was told to look for an iron weathercock with a crow perched upon its comb on the roof of the study house. Once upon a time the cock turned in the wind, but for years now it hasn't moved, not even in thunder and lightning. In Tishevitz, even iron weather-cocks die.

I speak in the present tense as for me time stands still. I arrive. I look around. For the life of me I can't find a single one of our men. The cemetery is empty. There is no outhouse. I go to the ritual bathhouse, but I don't hear a sound. I sit down on the highest bench, look down on the stone on which the buckets of water are poured each Friday, and wonder. Why am I needed here? If a little demon is wanted, is it necessary to import one all the way from Lublin? Aren't there enough devils in Zamosc? Outside the sun is shining – it's close to the summer solstice – but inside the bathhouse it's gloomy and cold. Above me is a spider web, and within the web a spider wiggling its legs, seeming to spin but drawing no thread. There's no sign of a fly, not even the shell of a fly. 'What does the creature eat?' I ask myself. 'Its own insides?' Suddenly I hear it chanting in a Talmudic singsong: 'A lion isn't satisfied by a morsel and a ditch isn't filled up with dirt from its own walls.'

I burst out laughing.

'Is that so? Why have you disguised yourself as a spider?'

'I've already been a worm, a flea, a frog. I've been sitting here for two hundred years without a stitch of work to do. But you need a permit to leave.'

'They don't sin here?'

'Petty men, petty sins. Today someone covets another man's broom; tomorrow he fasts and puts peas in his shoes. Ever since Abraham Zalman was under the illusion that he was Messiah, the son of Joseph, the blood of the people has congealed in their veins. If I were Satan, I wouldn't even send one of our first-graders here.'

'How much does it cost him?'

'What's new in the world?' he asks me.

'It's not been so good for our crowd.'

'What's happened? The Holy Spirit grows stronger?'

'Stronger? Only in Tishevitz is he powerful. No one's

3

heard of him in the large cities. Even in Lublin he's out of style.'

'Well, that should be fine.'

'But it isn't,' I said. ' "All-Guilty is worse for us than All-Innocent." It has reached a point where people want to sin beyond their capacities. They martyr themselves for the most trivial of sins. If that's the way it is, what are we needed for? A short while ago I was flying over Levertov Street, and I saw a man dressed in a skunk's coat. He had a black beard and wavy sidelocks; an amber cigar holder was clamped between his lips. Across the street from him an official's wife was walking, so it occurs to me to say, "That's quite a bargain, don't you think, Uncle?" All I expected from him was a thought. I had my handkerchief ready if he should spit on me. So what does the man do? "Why waste your breath on me?" he calls out angrily. "I'm willing. Start working on her." '

'What sort of a misfortune is this?'

'Enlightenment! In the two hundred years you've been sitting on your tail here, Satan has cooked up a new dish of kasha. The Jews have now developed writers. Yiddish ones, Hebrew ones, and they have taken over our trade. We grow hoarse talking to every adolescent, but they print their kitsch by the thousands and distribute it to Jews everywhere. They know all our tricks – mockery, piety. They have a hundred reasons why a rat must be kosher. All that they want to do is to redeem the world. Why, if you could corrupt nothing, have you been left here for two hundred years? And if you could do nothing in two hundred years, what do they expect from me in two weeks?'

'You know the proverb, "A guest for a while sees a mile."'

'What's there to see?'

'A young rabbi has moved here from Modly Bozyc. He's not yet thirty, but he's absolutely stuffed with knowledge, knows the thirty-six tractates of the Talmud by heart. He's the greatest Cabalist in Poland, fasts every Monday and Thursday, and bathes in the ritual bath when the water is ice cold. He won't permit any of us to talk to him. What's more he has a handsome wife, and that's bread in the basket. What do we have to tempt him with? You might as well try to break through an iron wall. If I were asked my opinion, I'd say that Tishevitz should be removed from our files. All I ask is that you get me out of here before I go mad.'

'No, first I must have a talk with this rabbi. How do you think I should start?'

'You tell me. He'll start pouring salt on your tail before you open your mouth.'

'I'm from Lublin. I'm not so easily frightened.'

II

On the way to the rabbi, I ask the imp, 'What have you tried so far?'

'What haven't I tried?' he answers.

'A woman?'

'Won't look at one.'

'Heresy?'

'He knows all the answers.'

'Money?'

'Doesn't know what a coin looks like.'

'Reputation?'

'He runs from it.'

'Doesn't he look backwards?'

'Doesn't even move his head.'

'He's got to have some angle.'

'Where's it hidden?'

The window of the rabbi's study is open, and in we fly. There's the usual paraphernalia around: an ark with the Holy Scroll, bookshelves, a mezuzah in a wooden case. The rabbi, a young man with a blond beard, blue eyes, yellow sidelocks, a high forehead, and a deep widow's peak sits on the rabbinical chair peering in the Gemara. He's fully equipped: yarmulka, sash, and fringed garment with each of the fringes braided eight times. I listen to his skull: pure thoughts! He sways and chants in Hebrew, '*Rachel t'unah v'gazezah*,' and then translates: 'A woolly sheep fleeced.'

'In Hebrew Rachel is both a sheep and a girl's name,' I say.

'So?'

'A sheep has wool and a girl has hair.'

'Therefore?'

'If she's not androgynous, a girl has pubic hair.'

'Stop babbling and let me study,' the rabbi says in anger.

'Wait a second,' I say. 'Torah won't get cold. It's true that Jacob loved Rachel, but when he was given Leah instead, she wasn't poison. And when Rachel gave him Bilhah as a concubine, what did Leah do to spite her sister? She put Zilpah into his bed.'

'That was before the giving of Torah.'

'What about King David?'

'That happened before the excommunication by Rabbi Gershom.'

'Before or after Rabbi Gershom, a male is a male.'

'Rascal. *Shaddai kra Satan*,' the rabbi exclaims. Grabbing both of his sidelocks, he begins to tremble as if assaulted by a bad dream. 'What nonsense am I thinking?' He takes his ear lobes and closes his ears. I keep on talking but he doesn't listen; he becomes absorbed in a

7

difficult passage and there's no longer anyone to speak to. The little imp from Tishevitz says, 'He's a hard one to hook, isn't he? Tomorrow he'll fast and roll in a bed of thistles. He'll give away his last penny to charity.'

'Such a believer nowadays?'

'Strong as a rock.'

'And his wife?'

'A sacrificial lamb.'

'What of the children?'

'Still infants.'

'Perhaps he has a mother-in-law?'

'She's already in the other world.'

'Any quarrels?'

'Not even half an enemy.'

'Where do you find such a jewel?'

'Once in a while something like that turns up among the Jews.'

'This one I've got to get. This is my first job around here. I've been promised that if I succeed, I'll be transferred to Odessa.'

'What's so good about that?'

'It's as near paradise as our kind gets. You can sleep twenty-four hours a day. The population sins and you don't lift a finger.'

'So what do you do all day?'

'We play with our women.'

'Here there's not a single one of our girls.' The imp sighs. 'There was one old bitch but she expired.'

'So what's left?'

'What Onan did.'

'That doesn't lead anywhere. Help me and I swear by Asmodeus's beard that I'll get you out of here. We have an opening for a mixer of bitter herbs. You only work Passovers.'

'I hope it works out, but don't count your chickens.'

'We've taken care of tougher than he.'

III

A week goes by and our business has not moved forward; I find myself in a dirty mood. A week in Tishevitz is equal to a year in Lublin. The Tishevitz imp is all right, but when you sit two hundred years in such a hole, you become a yokel. He cracks jokes that didn't amuse Enoch and convulses with laughter; he drops names from the Haggadah. Every one of his stories wears a long beard. I'd like to get the hell out of here, but it doesn't take a magician to return home with nothing. I have enemies among my colleagues and I must beware of intrigue. Perhaps I was sent here just to break my neck. When devils stop warring with people, they start tripping each other.

Experience has taught that of all the snares we use, there are three that work unfailingly – lust, pride, and avarice. No one can evade all three, not even Rabbi Tsots himself. Of the three, pride has the strongest meshes. According to the Talmud a scholar is permitted the eighth part of an eighth part of vanity. But a learned man generally exceeds his quota. When I see that the days are passing and that the rabbi of Tishevitz remains stubborn, I concentrate on vanity.

'Rabbi of Tishevitz,' I say, 'I wasn't born yesterday. I come from Lublin, where the streets are paved with exegeses of the Talmud. We use manuscripts to heat our ovens. The floors of our attics sag under the weight of Cabala. But not even in Lublin have I met a man of your eminence. How does it happen,' I ask, 'that no one's heard of you? True saints should hide themselves, perhaps, but silence will not bring redemption. You should be the leader of this generation, and not merely the rabbi of this community, holy though it is. The time has come for you to reveal yourself. Heaven and earth are waiting for you. Messiah himself sits in the Bird Nest looking down in search of an unblemished saint like you. But what are you doing about it? You sit on your rabbinical chair laying down the law on which pots and which pans are kosher. Forgive me the comparison, but it is as if an elephant were put to work hauling a straw.'

'Who are you and what do you want?' the rabbi asks in terror. 'Why don't you let me study?'

'There is a time when the service of God requires the neglect of Torah,' I scream. 'Any student can study the Gemara.'

'Who sent you here?'

'I was sent; I am here. Do you think they don't know about you up there? The higher-ups are annoyed with you. Broad shoulders must bear their share of the load. To put it in rhyme: the humble can stumble. Hearken to this: Abraham Zalman was Messiah, son of Joseph, and you are ordained to prepare the way for Messiah, son of David, but stop sleeping. Get ready for battle. The world sinks to the forty-ninth gate of uncleanliness, but you have broken through to the seventh firmament. Only one cry is heard in the mansions, the man from Tishevitz. The angel in charge of Edom has marshaled a clan of demons against you. Satan lies in wait also. Asmodeus is undermining you. Lilith and Namah hover at your bedside. You don't see them, but Shabriri and Briri are treading at your heels. If the Angels were not defending you, that unholy crowd would pound you to dust and ashes. But you do not stand alone, Rabbi of

Tishevitz. Lord Sandalphon guards your every step. Metratron watches over you from his luminescent sphere. Everything hangs in the balance, man of Tishevitz; you can tip the scales.'

'What should I do?'

'Mark well all that I tell you. Even if I command you to break the law, do as I bid.'

'Who are you? What is your name?'

'Elijah the Tishbite. I have the ram's horn of the Messiah ready. Whether the redemption comes, or we wander in the darkness of Egypt another 2,689 years is up to you.'

The rabbi of Tishevitz remains silent for a long time. His face becomes as white as the slips of paper on which he writes his commentaries.

'How do I know you're speaking the truth?' he asks in a trembling voice. 'Forgive me, Holy Angel, but I require a sign.'

'You are right. I will give you a sign.'

And I raise such a wind in the rabbi's study that the slip of paper on which he is writing rises from the table and starts flying like a pigeon. The pages of the Gemara turn by themselves. The curtain of the Holy Scroll billows. The rabbi's yarmulka jumps from his head, soars to the ceiling, and drops back onto his skull.

'Is that how Nature behaves?' I ask.

'No.'

'Do you believe me now?'

The rabbi of Tishevitz hesitates. 'What do you want me to do?'

'The leader of this generation must be famous.'

'How do you become famous?'

'Go and travel in the world.'

'What do I do in the world?'

'Preach and collect money.'

'For what do I collect?'

'First of all collect. Later on I'll tell you what to do with the money.'

'Who will contribute?'

'When I order, Jews give.'

'How will I support myself?'

'A rabbinical emissary is entitled to a part of what he collects.'

'And my family?'

'You will get enough for all.'

'What am I supposed to do right now?'

'Shut the Gemara.'

'Ah, but my soul yearns for Torah,' the rabbi of Tishevitz groans. Nevertheless, he lifts the cover of the book, ready to shut it. If he had done that, he would have been through. What did Joseph de la Rinah do? Just hand Samael a pinch of snuff. I am already laughing

13

to myself, 'Rabbi of Tishevitz, I have you all wrapped up.' The little bathhouse imp, standing in a corner, cocks an ear and turns green with envy. True, I have promised to do him a favor, but the jealousy of our kind is stronger than anything. Suddenly the rabbi says, 'Forgive me, my Lord, but I require another sign.'

'What do you want me to do? Stop the sun?'

'Just show me your feet.'

The moment the rabbi of Tishevitz speaks these words, I know everything is lost. We can disguise all the parts of our body but the feet. From the smallest imp right up to Ketev Meriri we all have the claws of geese. The little imp in the corner bursts out laughing. For the first time in a thousand years I, the master of speech, lose my tongue.

'I don't show my feet,' I call out in rage.

'That means you're a devil. *Pik*, get out of here,' the rabbi cries. He races to his bookcase, pulls out *The Book of Creation* and waves it menacingly over me. What devil can withstand *The Book of Creation*? I run from the rabbi's study with my spirit in pieces.

To make a long story short, I remain stuck in Tishevitz. No more Lublin, no more Odessa. In one second all my stratagems turn to ashes. An order comes from Asmodeus himself. 'Stay in Tishevitz and fry. Don't go further than a man is allowed to walk on the Sabbath.'

How long am I here? Eternity plus a Wednesday. I've seen it all, the destruction of Tishevitz, the destruction of Poland. There are no more Jews, no more demons. The women don't pour out water any longer on the night of the winter solstice. They don't avoid giving things in even numbers. They no longer knock at dawn at the antechamber of the synagogue. They don't warn us before emptying the slops. The rabbi was martyred on a Friday in the month of Nisan. The community was slaughtered, the holy books burned, the cemetery desecrated. *The Book of Creation* has been returned to the Creator. Gentiles wash themselves in the ritual bath. Abraham Zalman's chapel has been turned into a pigsty. There is no longer an Angel of Good or an Angel of Evil. No more sins, no more temptations! The generation is already guilty seven times over, but Messiah does not come. To whom should he come? Messiah did not come for the Jews, so the Jews went to Messiah. There is no further need for demons. We have also been annihilated. I am the last, a refugee. I can go anywhere I please, but where should a demon like me go? To the murderers?

I found a Yiddish storybook between two broken barrels in the house which once belonged to Velvel the barrelmaker. I sit there, the last of the demons. I eat dust. I sleep on a feather duster. I keep on reading gibberish. The style of the book is in our manner; Sabbath pudding cooked in pig's fat: blasphemy rolled in piety. The moral of the book is: neither judge, nor judgment. But nevertheless the letters are Jewish. The alphabet they could not squander. I suck on the letters and feed myself. I count the words, make rhymes, and tortuously interpret and reinterpret each dot.

> *Aleph*, the abyss, what else waited?
> *Beth*, the blow, long since fated.
> *Gimel*, God, pretending He knew,
> *Daleth*, death, its shadow grew.
> *Hai*, the hangman, he stood prepared;
> *Vov*, wisdom, ignorance bared.
> *Zayeen*, the zodiac, signs distantly loomed;
> *Chet*, the child, prenatally doomed.
> *Tet*, the thinker, an imprisoned lord;
> *Yud*, the judge, the verdict a fraud.

Yes, as long as a single volume remains, I have something to sustain me. As long as the moths have not destroyed the last page, there is something to play with. What will happen when the last letter is no more, I'd rather not bring to my lips.

> *When the last letter is gone,*
> *The last of the demons is done.*

Yentl the Yeshiva Boy

I

After her father's death, Yentl had no reason to remain in Yanev. She was all alone in the house. To be sure, lodgers were willing to move in and pay rent; and the marriage brokers flocked to her door with offers from Lublin, Tomashev, Zamosc. But Yentl didn't want to get married. Inside her, a voice repeated over and over: 'No!' What becomes of a girl when the wedding's over? Right away she starts bearing and rearing. And her mother-in-law lords it over her. Yentl knew she wasn't cut out for a woman's life. She couldn't sew, she couldn't knit. She let the food burn and the milk boil over; her Sabbath pudding never turned out right, and her hallah dough didn't rise. Yentl much preferred men's activities to women's. Her father, Reb Todros, may he rest in peace, during many bedridden years had studied Torah with his daughter as if she were a son. He told Yentl to

17

lock the doors and drape the windows, then together they pored over the Pentateuch, the Mishnah, the Gemara, and the Commentaries. She had proved so apt a pupil that her father used to say:

'Yentl – you have the soul of a man.'

'So why was I born a woman?'

'Even Heaven makes mistakes.'

There was no doubt about it, Yentl was unlike any of the girls in Yanev – tall, thin, bony, with small breasts and narrow hips. On Sabbath afternoons, when her father slept, she would dress up in his trousers, his fringed garment, his silk coat, his skullcap, his velvet hat, and study her reflection in the mirror. She looked like a dark, handsome young man. There was even a slight down on her upper lip. Only her thick braids showed her womanhood – and if it came to that, hair could always be shorn. Yentl conceived a plan and day and night she could think of nothing else. No, she had not been created for the noodle board and the pudding dish, for chattering with silly women and pushing for a place at the butcher's block. Her father had told her so many tales of yeshivas, rabbis, men of letters! Her head was full of Talmudic disputations, questions and answers, learned phrases. Secretly, she had even smoked her father's long pipe.

Yentl told the dealers she wanted to sell the house

and go to live in Kalish with an aunt. The neighborhood women tried to talk her out of it, and the marriage brokers said she was crazy, that she was more likely to make a good match right here in Yanev. But Yentl was obstinate. She was in such a rush that she sold the house to the first bidder, and let the furniture go for a song. All she realized from her inheritance was one hundred and forty rubles. Then late one night in the month of Av, while Yanev slept, Yentl cut off her braids, arranged sidelocks at her temples, and dressed herself in her father's clothes. Packing underclothes, phylacteries, and a few books into a straw suitcase, she started off on foot for Lublin.

On the main road, Yentl got a ride in a carriage that took her as far as Zamosc. From there, she again set out on foot. She stopped at an inn along the way, and gave her name there as Anshel, after an uncle who had died. The inn was crowded with young men journeying to study with famous rabbis. An argument was in progress over the merits of various yeshivas, some praising those of Lithuania, others claiming that study was more intensive in Poland and the board better. It was the first time Yentl had ever found herself alone in the company of young men. How different their talk was from the jabbering of women, she thought, but she was too shy to join in. One young man discussed a prospective match and the size of the dowry, while another, parodying the manner of a Purim rabbi, declaimed a passage from the Torah, adding all sorts of lewd interpretations. After a while, the company proceeded to contests of strength. One pried open another's fist; a second tried to bend a companion's arm. One student, dining on bread and tea, had no spoon and stirred his cup with his penknife.

Presently, one of the group came over to Yentl and poked her in the shoulder. 'Why so quiet? Don't you have a tongue?'

'I have nothing to say.'

'What's your name?'

'Anshel.'

'You *are* bashful. A violet by the wayside.'

And the young man tweaked Yentl's nose. She would have given him a smack in return, but her arm refused to budge. She turned white. Another student, slightly older than the rest, tall and pale, with burning eyes and a black beard, came to her rescue.

'Hey, you, why are you picking on him?'

'If you don't like it, you don't have to look.'

'Want me to pull your sidelocks off?'

The bearded young man beckoned to Yentl, then asked where she came from and where she was going.

Yentl told him she was looking for a yeshiva, but wanted a quiet one. The young man pulled at his beard.

'Then come with me to Bechev.'

He explained that he was returning to Bechev for his fourth year. The yeshiva there was small, with only thirty students, and the people in the town provided board for them all. The food was plentiful and the housewives darned the students' socks and took care of their laundry. The Bechev rabbi, who headed the yeshiva, was a genius. He could pose ten questions and answer all ten with one proof. Most of the students eventually found wives in the town.

'Why did you leave in the middle of the term?' Yentl asked.

'My mother died. Now I'm on my way back.'

'What's your name?'

'Avigdor.'

'How is it you're not married?'

The young man scratched his beard. 'It's a long story.'

'Tell me.'

Avigdor covered his eyes and thought a moment. 'Are you coming to Bechev?'

'Yes.'

'Then you'll find out soon enough anyway. I was

21

engaged to the only daughter of Alter Vishkower, the richest man in town. Even the wedding date was set when suddenly they sent back the engagement contract.'

'What happened?'

'I don't know. Gossips, I guess, were busy spreading tales. I had the right to ask for half the dowry, but it was against my nature. Now they're trying to talk me into another match, but the girl doesn't appeal to me.'

'In Bechev, yeshiva boys look at women?'

'At Alter's house, where I ate once a week, Hadass, his daughter, always brought in the food . . .'

'Is she good-looking?'

'She's blond.'

'Brunettes can be good-looking too.'

'No.'

Yentl gazed at Avigdor. He was lean and bony with sunken cheeks. He had curly sidelocks so black they appeared blue, and his eyebrows met across the bridge of his nose. He looked at her sharply with the regretful shyness of one who has just divulged a secret. His lapel was rent, according to the custom for mourners, and the lining of his gaberdine showed through. He drummed restlessly on the table and hummed a tune. Behind the high furrowed brow his thoughts seemed to race. Suddenly he spoke:

'Well, what of it. I'll become a recluse, that's all.'

II

It was strange, but as soon as Yentl – or Anshel – arrived in Bechev, she was allotted one day's board a week at the house of that same rich man, Alter Vishkower, whose daughter had broken off her betrothal to Avigdor.

The students at the yeshiva studied in pairs, and Avigdor chose Anshel for a partner. He helped her with the lessons. He was also an expert swimmer and offered to teach Anshel the breast stroke and how to tread water, but she always found excuses for not going down to the river. Avigdor suggested that they share lodgings, but Anshel found a place to sleep at the house of an elderly widow who was half blind. Tuesdays, Anshel ate at Alter Vishkower's and Hadass waited on her. Avigdor always asked many questions: 'How does Hadass look? Is she sad? Is she gay? Are they trying to marry her off? Does she ever mention my name?' Anshel reported that Hadass upset dishes on the tablecloth, forgot to bring the salt, and dipped her fingers into the plate of grits while carrying it. She ordered the servant girl around, was forever engrossed in storybooks, and changed her hairdo every week. Moreover, she must consider herself a beauty, for she was always in front of the mirror, but, in fact, she was not that good-looking.

'Two years after she's married,' said Anshel, 'she'll be an old bag.'

'So she doesn't appeal to you?'

'Not particularly.'

'Yet if she wanted you, you wouldn't turn her down.'

'I can do without her.'

'Don't you have evil impulses?'

The two friends, sharing a lectern in a corner of the study house, spent more time talking than learning. Occasionally Avigdor smoked, and Anshel, taking the cigarette from his lips, would have a puff. Avigdor liked baked flatcakes made with buckwheat, so Anshel stopped at the bakery every morning to buy one, and wouldn't let him pay his share. Often Anshel did things that greatly surprised Avigdor. If a button came off Avigdor's coat, for example, Anshel would arrive at the yeshiva the next day with needle and thread and sew it back on. Anshel bought Avigdor all kinds of presents: a silk handkerchief, a pair of socks, a muffler. Avigdor grew more and more attached to this boy, five years younger than himself, whose beard hadn't even begun to sprout.

Once Avigdor said to Anshel: 'I want you to marry Hadass.'

'What good would that do *you*?'

'Better you than a total stranger.'

'You'd become my enemy.'

'Never.'

Avigdor liked to go for walks through the town and Anshel frequently joined him. Engrossed in conversation, they would go off to the water mill, or to the pine forest, or to the crossroads where the Christian shrine stood. Sometimes they stretched out on the grass.

'Why can't a woman be like a man?' Avigdor asked once, looking up at the sky.

'How do you mean?'

'Why couldn't Hadass be just like you?'

'How like me?'

'Oh – a good fellow.'

Anshel grew playful. She plucked a flower and tore off the petals one by one. She picked up a chestnut and threw it at Avigdor. Avigdor watched a ladybug crawl across the palm of his hand.

After a while he spoke up: 'They're trying to marry me off.'

Anshel sat up instantly. 'To whom?'

'To Feitl's daughter, Peshe.'

'The widow?'

'That's the one.'

'Why should you marry a widow?'

'No one else will have me.'

25

'That's not true. Someone will turn up for you.'

'Never.'

Anshel told Avigdor such a match was bad. Peshe was neither good-looking nor clever, only a cow with a pair of eyes. Besides, she was bad luck, for her husband died in the first year of their marriage. Such women were husband-killers. But Avigdor did not answer. He lit a cigarette, took a deep puff, and blew out smoke rings. His face had turned green.

'I need a woman. I can't sleep at night.'

Anshel was startled. 'Why can't you wait until the right one comes along?'

'Hadass was my destined one.'

And Avigdor's eyes grew moist. Abruptly he got to his feet. 'Enough lying around. Let's go.'

After that, everything happened quickly. One day Avigdor was confiding his problem to Anshel, two days later he became engaged to Peshe, and brought honey cake and brandy to the yeshiva. An early wedding date was set. When the bride-to-be is a widow, there's no need to wait for a trousseau. Everything is ready. The groom, moreover, was an orphan and no one's advice had to be asked. The yeshiva students drank the brandy and offered their congratulations. Anshel also took a sip, but promptly choked on it.

'Oy, it burns!'

'You're not much of a man,' Avigdor teased.

After the celebration, Avigdor and Anshel sat down with a volume of the Gemara, but they made little progress, and their conversation was equally slow. Avigdor rocked back and forth, pulled at his beard, muttered under his breath.

'I'm lost,' he said abruptly.

'If you don't like her, why are you getting married?'

'I'd marry a she-goat.'

The following day Avigdor did not appear at the study house. Feitl the leather dealer belonged to the Hasidim and he wanted his prospective son-in-law to continue his studies at the Hasidic prayer house. The yeshiva students said privately that though there was no denying the widow was short and round as a barrel, her mother the daughter of a dairyman, her father half an ignoramus, still the whole family was filthy with money. Feitl was part-owner of a tannery; Peshe had invested her dowry in a shop that sold herring, tar, pots and pans, and was always crowded with peasants. Father and daughter were outfitting Avigdor and had placed orders for a fur coat, a cloth coat, a silk kapote, and two pair of boots. In addition, he had received many gifts immediately, things that had belonged to Peshe's first husband: the Vilna edition of the Talmud, a gold watch, a Hanukkah candelabra, a spice box. Anshel sat alone at the lectern.

On Tuesday when Anshel arrived for dinner at Alter Vishkower's house, Hadass remarked: 'What do you say about your partner – back in clover, isn't he?'

'What did you expect – that no one else would want him?'

Hadass reddened. 'It wasn't my fault. My father was against it.'

'Why?'

'Because they found out a brother of his had hanged himself.'

Anshel looked at her as she stood there – tall, blond, with a long neck, hollow cheeks, and blue eyes, wearing a cotton dress and a calico apron. Her hair, fixed in two braids, was flung back over her shoulders. A pity I'm not a man, Anshel thought.

'Do you regret it now?' Anshel asked.

'Oh, yes!'

Hadass fled from the room. The rest of the food, meat dumplings and tea, was brought in by the servant girl. Not until Anshel had finished eating and was washing her hands for the Final Blessings did Hadass reappear.

She came up to the table and said in a smothered voice: 'Swear to me you won't tell him anything. Why should he know what goes on in my heart!'

Then she fled once more, nearly falling over the threshold.

III

The head of the yeshiva asked Anshel to choose another
study partner, but weeks went by and still Anshel studied alone. There was no one in the yeshiva who could
take Avigdor's place. All the others were small, in body
and in spirit. They talked nonsense, bragged about
trifles, grinned oafishly, behaved like shnorrers. Without Avigdor the study house seemed empty. At night
Anshel lay on her bench at the widow's, unable to sleep.
Stripped of gaberdine and trousers, she was once more
Yentl, a girl of marriageable age, in love with a young
man who was betrothed to another. Perhaps I should
have told him the truth, Anshel thought. But it was too
late for that. Anshel could not go back to being a girl,
could never again do without books and a study house.
She lay there thinking outlandish thoughts that brought
her close to madness. She fell asleep, then awoke with a
start. In her dream she had been at the same time a man
and a woman, wearing both a woman's bodice and a
man's fringed garment. Yentl's period was late and she
was suddenly afraid . . . who knew? In *Medrash Talpioth*
she had read of a woman who had conceived merely
through desiring a man. Only now did Yentl grasp the
meaning of the Torah's prohibition against wearing the

29

clothes of the other sex. By doing so one deceived not only others but also oneself. Even the soul was perplexed, finding itself incarnate in a strange body.

At night Anshel lay awake; by day she could scarcely keep her eyes open. At the houses where she had her meals, the women complained that the youth left everything on his plate. The rabbi noticed that Anshel no longer paid attention to the lectures but stared out the window lost in private thoughts. When Tuesday came, Anshel appeared at the Vishkower house for dinner. Hadass set a bowl of soup before her and waited, but Anshel was so disturbed she did not even say thank you. She reached for a spoon but let it fall.

Hadass ventured a comment: 'I hear Avigdor has deserted you.'

Anshel awoke from her trance. 'What do you mean?'

'He's no longer your partner.'

'He's left the yeshiva.'

'Do you see him at all?'

'He seems to be hiding.'

'Are you at least going to the wedding?'

For a moment Anshel was silent as though missing the meaning of the words. Then she spoke: 'He's a big fool.'

'Why do you say that?'

'You're beautiful, and the other one looks like a monkey.'

Hadass blushed to the roots of her hair. 'It's all my father's fault.'

'Don't worry. You'll find someone who's worthy of you.'

'There's no one I want.'

'But everyone wants you . . .'

There was a long silence. Hadass's eyes grew larger, filling with the sadness of one who knows there is no consolation.

'Your soup is getting cold.'

'I, too, want you.'

Anshel was astonished at what she had said. Hadass stared at her over her shoulder.

'What are you saying!'

'It's the truth.'

'Someone might be listening.'

'I'm not afraid.'

'Eat the soup. I'll bring the meat dumplings in a moment.'

Hadass turned to go, her high heels clattering. Anshel began hunting for beans in the soup, fished one up, then let it fall. Her appetite was gone; her throat had closed up. She knew very well she was getting entangled in evil, but some force kept urging her on. Hadass reappeared, carrying a platter with two meat dumplings on it.

'Why aren't you eating?'

'I'm thinking about you.'

'What are you thinking?'

'I want to marry you.'

Hadass made a face as though she had swallowed something.

'On such matters, you must speak to my father.'

'I know.'

'The custom is to send a matchmaker.'

She ran from the room, letting the door slam behind her. Laughing inwardly, Anshel thought: 'With girls I can play as I please!' She sprinkled salt on the soup and then pepper. She sat there lightheaded. What have I done? I must be going mad. There's no other explanation . . . She forced herself to eat, but could taste nothing. Only then did Anshel remember that it was Avigdor who had wanted her to marry Hadass. From her confusion, a plan emerged; she would exact vengeance for Avigdor, and at the same time, through Hadass, draw him closer to herself. Hadass was a virgin: what did she know about men? A girl like that could be deceived for a long time. To be sure, Anshel too was a virgin but she knew a lot about such matters from the Gemara and from hearing men talk. Anshel was seized by both fear and glee, as a person is who is planning to deceive the whole community. She remembered the saying: 'The public are fools.' She stood up and said aloud: 'Now I'll really start something.'

That night Anshel didn't sleep a wink. Every few minutes she got up for a drink of water. Her throat was parched, her forehead burned. Her brain worked away feverishly of its own volition. A quarrel seemed to be going on inside her. Her stomach throbbed and her knees ached. It was as if she had sealed a pact with Satan, the Evil One who plays tricks on human beings, who sets stumbling blocks and traps in their paths. By the time Anshel fell asleep, it was morning. She awoke more exhausted than before. But she could not go on sleeping on the bench at the widow's. With an effort she rose and, taking the bag that held her phylacteries, set out for the study house. On the way whom should she meet but Hadass's father. Anshel bade him a respectful good morning and received a friendly greeting in return. Reb Alter stroked his beard and engaged her in conversation:

'My daughter Hadass must be serving you left-overs. You look starved.'

'Your daughter is a fine girl, and very generous.'

'So why are you so pale?'

Anshel was silent for a minute. 'Reb Alter, there's something I must say to you.'

'Well, go ahead, say it.'

33

'Reb Alter, your daughter pleases me.'

Alter Vishkower came to a halt. 'Oh, does she? I thought yeshiva students didn't talk about such things.'

His eyes were full of laughter.

'But it's the truth.'

'One doesn't discuss these matters with the young man himself.'

'But I'm an orphan.'

'Well . . . in that case the custom is to send a marriage broker.'

'Yes . . .'

'What do you see in her?'

'She's beautiful . . . fine . . . intelligent . . .'

'Well, well, well . . . Come along, tell me something about your family.'

Alter Vishkower put his arm around Anshel and in this fashion the two continued walking until they reached the courtyard of the synagogue.

IV

Once you say 'A,' you must say 'B.' Thoughts lead to words, words lead to deeds. Reb Alter Vishkower gave his consent to the match. Hadass's mother Freyda Leah held back for a while. She said she wanted no more

Bechev yeshiva students for her daughter and would rather have someone from Lublin or Zamosc; but Hadass gave warning that if she were shamed publicly once more (the way she had been with Avigdor) she would throw herself into the well. As often happens with such ill-advised matches, everyone was strongly in favor of it – the rabbi, the relatives, Hadass's girl friends. For some time the girls of Bechev had been eyeing Anshel longingly, watching from their windows when the youth passed by on the street. Anshel kept his boots well polished and did not drop his eyes in the presence of women. Stopping in at Beila the baker's to buy a *pletzl*, he joked with them in such a worldly fashion that they marveled. The women agreed there was something special about Anshel: his sidelocks curled like nobody else's and he tied his neck scarf differently; his eyes, smiling yet distant, seemed always fixed on some faraway point. And the fact that Avigdor had become betrothed to Feitl's daughter Peshe, forsaking Anshel, had endeared him all the more to the people of the town. Alter Vishkower had a provisional contract drawn up for the betrothal, promising Anshel a bigger dowry, more presents, and an even longer period of maintenance than he had promised Avigdor. The girls of Bechev threw their arms around Hadass and congratulated her. Hadass immediately began crocheting a sack for

Anshel's phylacteries, a hallah cloth, a matzoh bag. When Avigdor heard the news of Anshel's betrothal, he came to the study house to offer his congratulations. The past few weeks had aged him. His beard was disheveled, his eyes were red.

He said to Anshel: 'I knew it would happen this way. Right from the beginning. As soon as I met you at the inn.'

'But it was you who suggested it.'

'I know that.'

'Why did you desert me? You went away without even saying goodbye.'

'I wanted to burn my bridges behind me.'

Avigdor asked Anshel to go for a walk. Though it was already past Succoth, the day was bright with sunshine. Avigdor, friendlier than ever, opened his heart to Anshel. Yes, it was true, a brother of his had succumbed to melancholy and hanged himself. Now he too felt himself near the edge of the abyss. Peshe had a lot of money and her father was a rich man, yet he couldn't sleep nights. He didn't want to be a storekeeper. He couldn't forget Hadass. She appeared in his dreams. Sabbath night when her name occurred in the Havdala prayer, he turned dizzy. Still it was good that Anshel and no one else was to marry her . . . At least she would fall into decent hands. Avigdor stooped and tore aimlessly at the shriveled grass. His speech was incoherent, like that of a man possessed.

Suddenly he said: 'I have thought of doing what my brother did.'

'Do you love her *that* much?'

'She's engraved in my heart.'

The two pledged their friendship and promised never again to part. Anshel proposed that, after they were both married, they should live next door or even share the same house. They would study together every day, perhaps even become partners in a shop.

'Do you want to know the truth?' asked Avigdor. 'It's like the story of Jacob and Benjamin: my life is bound up in your life.'

'Then why did you leave me?'

'Perhaps for that very reason.'

Though the day had turned cold and windy, they continued to walk until they reached the pine forest, not turning back until dusk when it was time for the evening prayer. The girls of Bechev, from their posts at the windows, watched them going by with their arms round each other's shoulders and so engrossed in conversation that they walked through puddles and piles of trash without noticing. Avigdor looked pale, disheveled, and the wind whipped one sidelock about; Anshel chewed his fingernails. Hadass, too, ran to the window, took one look, and her eyes filled with tears.

Events followed quickly. Avigdor was the first to marry. Because the bride was a widow, the wedding was a quiet one, with no musicians, no wedding jester, no ceremonial veiling of the bride. One day Peshe stood beneath the marriage canopy, the next she was back at the shop, dispensing tar with greasy hands. Avigdor prayed at the Hasidic assembly house in his new prayer shawl. Afternoons, Anshel went to visit him and the two whispered and talked until evening. The date of Anshel's wedding to Hadass was set for the Sabbath in Hanukkah week, though the prospective father-in-law wanted it sooner. Hadass had already been betrothed once. Besides, the groom was an orphan. Why should he toss about on a makeshift bed at the widow's when he could have a wife and home of his own?

Many times each day Anshel warned herself that what she was about to do was sinful, mad, an act of utter depravity. She was entangling both Hadass and herself in a chain of deception and committing so many transgressions that she would never be able to do penance. One lie followed another. Repeatedly Anshel made up her mind to flee Bechev in time, to put an end to this weird comedy that was more the work of an imp than a human being. But she was in the grip of a power she could not resist. She grew more and more attached to Avigdor, and could not bring herself to destroy Hadass's illusory happiness. Now that he was married, Avigdor's desire to study was greater than ever, and the friends met twice each day: in the mornings they studied the Gemara and the Commentaries, in the afternoons the Legal Codes with their glosses. Alter Vishkower and Feitl the leather dealer were pleased and compared Avigdor and Anshel to David and Jonathan. With all the complications, Anshel went about as though drunk. The tailors took her measurements for a new wardrobe and she was forced into all kinds of subterfuge to keep them from discovering she was not a man. Though the imposture had lasted many weeks, Anshel still could not believe it. How was it possible? Fooling the community had become a game, but how long could it go on? And in what way would the truth come to the surface? Inside, Anshel laughed and wept. She had turned into a sprite brought into the world to mock people and trick them. I'm wicked, a transgressor, a Jeroboam ben Nabat, she told herself. Her only justification was that she had taken all these burdens upon herself because her soul thirsted to study Torah.

Avigdor soon began to complain that Peshe treated him badly. She called him an idler, a shlemiel, just another mouth to feed. She tried to tie him to the store, assigned him tasks for which he hadn't the slightest inclination, begrudged him pocket money. Instead of consoling Avigdor, Anshel goaded him on against Peshe. She called his wife an eyesore, a shrew, a miser, and said that Peshe had no doubt nagged her first husband to death and would Avigdor also. At the same time, Anshel enumerated Avigdor's virtues: his height and manliness, his wit, his erudition.

'If I were a woman and married to you,' said Anshel, 'I'd know how to appreciate you.'

'Well, but you aren't . . .'

Avigdor sighed.

Meanwhile, Anshel's wedding date drew near.

On the Sabbath before Hanukkah, Anshel was called to the pulpit to read from the Torah. The women showered her with raisins and almonds. On the day of the wedding Alter Vishkower gave a feast for the young men. Avigdor sat at Anshel's right hand. The bridegroom delivered a Talmudic discourse, and the rest of the company argued the points, while smoking cigarettes and drinking wine, liqueurs, tea with lemon or raspberry jam. Then followed the ceremony of veiling the bride, after which the bridegroom was led to the wedding canopy that had been set up at the side of the synagogue. The night was frosty and clear, the sky full of stars. The musicians struck up a tune. Two rows of girls held lighted tapers and braided wax candles. After the wedding ceremony the bride and groom broke their fast with golden chicken broth. Then the dancing began and the announcement of the wedding gifts, all according to custom. The gifts were many and costly. The wedding jester depicted the joys and sorrows that were in store for the bride. Avigdor's wife, Peshe, was one of the guests but, though she was bedecked with jewels, she still looked ugly in a wig that sat low on her forehead, wearing an enormous fur cape, and with traces of tar on her hands that no amount of washing could ever remove. After the virtue dance the bride and groom were led separately to the marriage chamber. The wedding attendants instructed the couple in the proper conduct and enjoined them to 'be fruitful and multiply.'

At daybreak Anshel's mother-in-law and her band descended upon the marriage chamber and tore the bedsheets from beneath Hadass to make sure the marriage had been consummated. When traces of blood were discovered, the company grew merry and began kissing and congratulating the bride. Then, brandishing the sheet, they flocked outside and danced a kosher dance in the newly fallen snow. Anshel had found a way to deflower the bride. Hadass in her innocence was unaware that things weren't quite as they should have been. She was already deeply in love with Anshel. It is commanded that the bride and groom remain apart for seven days after the first intercourse. The next day Anshel and Avigdor took up the study of the Tractate on Menstruous Women. When the other men had departed and the two were left to themselves in the synagogue, Avigdor shyly questioned Anshel about his night with Hadass. Anshel gratified his curiosity and they whispered together until nightfall.

V

Anshel had fallen into good hands. Hadass was a devoted wife and her parents indulged their son-in-law's every wish and boasted of his accomplishments. To be sure, several months went by and Hadass was still not with child, but no one took it to heart. On the other hand, Avigdor's lot grew steadily worse. Peshe tormented him and finally would not give him enough to eat and even refused him a clean shirt. Since he was always penniless, Anshel again brought him a daily buckwheat cake. Because Peshe was too busy to cook and too stingy to hire a servant, Anshel asked Avigdor to dine at his house. Reb Alter Vishkower and his wife disapproved, arguing that it was wrong for the rejected suitor to visit the house of his former fiancée. The town had plenty to talk about. But Anshel cited precedents to show that it was not prohibited by the Law. Most of the towns-people sided with Avigdor and blamed Peshe for everything. Avigdor soon began pressing Peshe for a divorce, and, because he did not want to have a child by such a fury, he acted like Onan, or, as the Gemara trans-lates it: he threshed on the inside and cast his seed without. He confided in Anshel, told him how Peshe came to bed unwashed and snored like a buzz saw, of how she was so occupied with the cash taken in at the store that she babbled about it even in her sleep.

'Oh, Anshel, how I envy you,' he said.

'There's no reason for envying me.'

'You have everything. I wish your good fortune were mine – with no loss to you, of course.'

'Everyone has troubles of his own.'

'What sort of troubles do *you* have? Don't tempt Providence.'

How could Avigdor have guessed that Anshel could not sleep at night and thought constantly of running away? Lying with Hadass and deceiving her had become more and more painful. Hadass's love and tenderness shamed her. The devotion of her mother- and father-in-law and their hopes for a grandchild were a burden. On

Friday afternoons all of the townspeople went to the baths and every week Anshel had to find a new excuse. But this was beginning to awake suspicions. There was talk that Anshel must have an unsightly birthmark, or a rupture, or perhaps was not properly circumcised. Judging by the youth's years, his beard should certainly have begun to sprout, yet his cheeks remained smooth. It was already Purim, and Passover was approaching. Soon it would be summer. Not far from Bechev there was a river where all the yeshiva students and young men went swimming as soon as it was warm enough. The lie was swelling like an abscess and one of these days it must surely burst. Anshel knew she had to find a way to free herself.

It was customary for the young men boarding with their in-laws to travel to nearby cities during the half-holidays in the middle of Passover week. They enjoyed the change, refreshed themselves, looked around for business opportunities, bought books or other things a young man might need. Bechev was not far from Lublin and Anshel persuaded Avigdor to make the journey with her at her expense. Avigdor was delighted at the prospect of being rid for a few days of the shrew he had at home. The trip by carriage was a merry one. The fields were turning green; storks, back from the warm countries, swooped across the sky in great arcs. Streams rushed toward the valleys. The birds chirped. The wind-mills turned. Spring flowers were beginning to bloom in the fields. Here and there a cow was already grazing. The companions, chatting, ate the fruit and little cakes that Hadass had packed, told each other jokes, and exchanged confidences until they reached Lublin. There they went to an inn and took a room for two. In the journey, Anshel had promised to reveal an astonishing secret to Avigdor in Lublin. Avigdor had joked: what sort of secret could it be? Had Anshel discovered a hidden treasure? Had he written an essay? By studying the Cabala, had he created a dove?

Now they entered the room and while Anshel carefully locked the door, Avigdor said teasingly: 'Well, let's hear your great secret.'

'Prepare yourself for the most incredible thing that ever was.'

'I'm prepared for anything.'

'I'm not a man but a woman,' said Anshel. 'My name isn't Anshel, it's Yentl.'

Avigdor burst out laughing. 'I knew it was a hoax.'

'But it's true.'

'Even if I'm a fool, I won't swallow this.'

'Do you want me to show you?'

'Yes.'

'Then I'll get undressed.'

45

Avigdor's eyes widened. It occurred to him that Anshel might want to practice pederasty. Anshel took off the gaberdine and the fringed garment, and threw off her underclothes. Avigdor took one look and turned first white, then fiery red. Anshel covered herself hastily.

'I've done this only so that you can testify at the courthouse. Otherwise, Hadass will have to stay a grass widow.'

Avigdor had lost his tongue. He was seized by a fit of trembling. He wanted to speak, but his lips moved and nothing came out. He sat down quickly, for his legs would not support him.

Finally he murmured: 'How is it possible? I don't believe it!'

'Should I get undressed again?'

'No!'

Yentl proceeded to tell the whole story: how her father, bedridden, had studied Torah with her; how she had never had the patience for women and their silly chatter; how she had sold the house and all the furnishings, left the town, made her way disguised as a man to Lublin, and on the road met Avigdor. Avigdor sat speechless, gazing at the storyteller. Yentl was by now wearing men's clothes once more.

Avigdor spoke: 'It must be a dream.'

He pinched himself on the cheek.

'It isn't a dream.'

'That such a thing should happen to me!'

'It's all true.'

'Why did you do it? *Nu*, I'd better keep still.'

'I didn't want to waste my life on a baking shovel and a kneading trough.'

'And what about Hadass – why did you do that?'

'I did it for your sake. I knew that Peshe would torment you and at our house you would have some peace.'

Avigdor was silent for a long time. He bowed his head, pressed his hands to his temples, shook his head. 'What will you do now?'

'I'll go away to a different yeshiva.'

'What? If you had only told me earlier, we could have . . .'

Avigdor broke off in the middle.

'No – it wouldn't have been good.'

'Why not?'

'I'm neither one nor the other.'

'What a dilemma I'm in!'

'Get a divorce from that horror. Marry Hadass.'

'She'll never divorce me and Hadass won't have me.'

'Hadass loves you. She won't listen to her father again.'

Avigdor stood up suddenly but then sat down. 'I won't be able to forget you. Ever . . .'

VI

According to the Law, Avigdor was now forbidden to spend another moment alone with Yentl; yet dressed in the gaberdine and trousers, she was again the familiar Anshel.

They resumed their conversation on the old footing: 'How could you bring yourself to violate the commandment every day: "A woman shall not wear that which pertaineth to a man"?'

'I wasn't created for plucking feathers and chattering with females.'

'Would you rather lose your share in the world to come?'

'Perhaps . . .'

Avigdor raised his eyes. Only now did he realize that Anshel's cheeks were too smooth for a man's, the hair too abundant, the hands too small. Even so he could not believe that such a thing could have happened. At any moment he expected to wake up. He bit his lips, pinched his thigh. He was seized by shyness and could not speak without stammering. His friendship with

Anshel, their intimate talk, their confidences, had been turned into a sham and delusion. The thought even occurred to him that Anshel might be a demon. He shook himself as if to cast off a nightmare; yet that power which knows the difference between dream and reality told him it was all true. He summoned up his courage. He and Anshel could never be strangers to one another, even though Anshel was in fact Yentl . . .

He ventured a comment: 'It seems to me that the witness who testifies for a deserted woman may not marry her, for the Law calls him "a party to the affair." '

'What? That didn't occur to me!'

'We must look it up in Eben Ezer.'

'I'm not even sure that the rules pertaining to a deserted woman apply in this case,' said Anshel in the manner of a scholar.

'If you don't want Hadass to be a grass widow, you must reveal the secret to her directly.'

'That I can't do.'

'In any event, you must get another witness.'

Gradually the two went back to their Talmudic conversation. It seemed strange at first to Avigdor to be disputing holy writ with a woman, yet before long the Torah had reunited them. Though their bodies were different, their souls were of one kind. Anshel spoke in a singsong, gesticulated with her thumb, clutched her sidelocks, plucked at her beardless chin, made all the customary gestures of a yeshiva student. In the heat of argument she even seized Avigdor by the lapel and called him stupid. A great love for Anshel took hold of Avigdor, mixed with shame, remorse, anxiety. If I had only known this before, he said to himself. In his thoughts he likened Anshel (or Yentl) to Bruria, the wife of Reb Meir, and to Yalta, the wife of Reb Nachman. For the first time he saw clearly that this was what he had always wanted: a wife whose mind was not taken up with material things . . . His desire for Hadass was gone now, and he knew he would long for Yentl, but he dared not say so. He felt hot and knew that his face was burning. He could no longer meet Anshel's eyes. He began to enumerate Anshel's sins and saw that he too was implicated, for he had sat next to Yentl and had touched her during her unclean days. *Nu*, and what could be said about her marriage to Hadass? What a multitude of transgressions there! Wilful deception, false vows, misrepresentation! – Heaven knows what else.

He asked suddenly: 'Tell the truth, are you a heretic?'

'God forbid!'

'Then how could you bring yourself to do such a thing?'

The longer Anshel talked, the less Avigdor understood. All Anshel's explanations seemed to point to one thing: she had the soul of a man and the body of a woman. Anshel said she had married Hadass only in order to be near Avigdor.

'You could have married me,' Avigdor said.

'I wanted to study the Gemara and Commentaries with you, not darn your socks!'

For a long time neither spoke. Then Avigdor broke the silence: 'I'm afraid Hadass will get sick from all this, God forbid!'

'I'm afraid of that, too.'

'What's going to happen now?'

Dusk fell and the two began to recite the evening prayer. In his confusion Avigdor mixed up the blessings, omitted some and repeated others. He glanced sideways at Anshel, who was rocking back and forth, beating her breast, bowing her head. He saw her, eyes closed, lift her face to Heaven, as though beseeching: You, Father in Heaven, know the truth . . . When their prayers were finished, they sat down on opposite chairs, facing one another yet a good distance apart. The room filled with shadows. Reflections of the sunset, like purple embroidery, shook on the wall opposite the window. Avigdor again wanted to speak but at first the words, trembling on the tip of his tongue, would not come.

Suddenly they burst forth: 'Maybe it's still not too late? I can't go on living with that accursed woman . . . You . . .'

'No, Avigdor, it's impossible.'

'Why?'

'I'll live out my time as I am . . .'

'I'll miss you. Terribly.'

'And I'll miss you.'

'What's the sense of all this?'

Anshel did not answer. Night fell and the light faded. In the darkness they seemed to be listening to each other's thoughts. The Law forbade Avigdor to stay in the room alone with Anshel, but he could not think of her just as a woman. What a strange power there is in clothing, he thought.

But he spoke of something else: 'I would advise you simply to send Hadass a divorce.'

'How can I do that?'

'Since the marriage sacraments weren't valid, what difference does it make?'

'I suppose you're right.'

'There'll be time enough later for her to find out the truth.'

The maidservant came in with a lamp, but as soon as she had gone, Avigdor put it out. Their predicament and the words which they must speak to one another could not endure light. In the blackness Anshel related all the particulars. She answered all Avigdor's questions. The clock struck two, and still they talked. Anshel told Avigdor that Hadass had never forgotten him. She talked of him frequently, worried about his health, was sorry – though not without a certain satisfaction – about the way things had turned out with Peshe.

'She'll be a good wife,' said Anshel. 'I don't even know how to bake a pudding.'

'Nevertheless, if you're willing . . .'

'No, Avigdor. It wasn't destined to be . . .'

VII

It was all a great riddle to the town: the messenger who arrived bringing Hadass the divorce papers; Avigdor's remaining in Lublin until after the holidays; his return to Bechev with slumping shoulders and lifeless eyes as if he had been ill. Hadass took to her bed and was visited by the doctor three times a day. Avigdor went into seclusion. If someone ran across him by chance and addressed him, he did not answer. Peshe complained to her parents that Avigdor paced back and forth smoking all night long. When he finally collapsed from sheer fatigue, in his sleep he called out the name of an unknown female – Yentl. Peshe began talking of a divorce. The town thought Avigdor wouldn't grant her one or would demand money at the very least, but he agreed to everything.

In Bechev the people were not used to having mysteries stay mysteries for long. How can you keep secrets in a little town where everyone knows what's cooking in everyone else's pots? Yet, though there were plenty of persons who made a practice of looking through keyholes and laying an ear to shutters, what happened remained an enigma. Hadass lay in her bed and wept. Chanina the herb doctor reported that she was wasting away. Anshel had disappeared without a trace. Reb Alter Vishkower sent for Avigdor and he arrived, but those who stood straining beneath the window couldn't catch a word of what passed between them. Those individuals who habitually pry into other people's affairs came up with all sorts of theories, but not one of them was consistent.

One party came to the conclusion that Anshel had fallen into the hands of Catholic priests and had been converted. That might have made sense. But where could Anshel have found time for the priests, since he was always studying in the yeshiva? And apart from that, since when does an apostate send his wife a divorce?

Another group whispered that Anshel had cast an eye on another woman. But who could it be? There were no love affairs conducted in Bechev. And none of the young women had recently left town – neither a Jewish woman nor a Gentile one.

Somebody else offered the suggestion that Anshel had been carried away by evil spirits, or was even one of them himself. As proof he cited the fact that Anshel had never come either to the bathhouse or to the river. It is well known that demons have the feet of geese. Well, but had Hadass never seen him barefoot? And who ever heard of a demon sending his wife a divorce? When a demon marries a daughter of mortals, he usually lets her remain a grass widow.

It occurred to someone else that Anshel had committed a major transgression and gone into exile in order to do penance. But what sort of transgression could it have been? And why had he not entrusted it to the rabbi? And why did Avigdor wander about like a ghost?

The hypothesis of Tevel the musician was closest to the truth. Tevel maintained that Avigdor had been unable to forget Hadass and that Anshel had divorced her so that his friend would be able to marry her. But was such friendship possible in this world? And in that case, why had Anshel divorced Hadass even before

Avigdor divorced Peshe? Furthermore, such a thing can be accomplished only if the wife has been informed of the arrangement and is willing, yet all signs pointed to Hadass's great love for Anshel, and in fact she was ill from sorrow.

One thing was clear to all: Avigdor knew the truth. But it was impossible to get anything out of him. He remained in seclusion and kept silent with an obstinacy that was a reproof to the whole town.

Close friends urged Peshe not to divorce Avigdor, though they had severed all relations and no longer lived as man and wife. He did not even, on Friday night, perform the kiddush blessing for her. He spent his nights either at the study house or at the widow's where Anshel had found lodgings. When Peshe spoke to him he didn't answer, but stood with bowed head. The tradeswoman Peshe had no patience for such goings-on. She needed a young man to help her out in the store, not a yeshiva student who had fallen into melancholy. Someone of that sort might even take it into his head to depart and leave her deserted. Peshe agreed to a divorce.

In the meantime, Hadass had recovered, and Reb Alter Vishkower let it be known that a marriage contract was being drawn up. Hadass was to marry Avigdor. The town was agog. A marriage between a man and a woman who had once been engaged and their betrothal broken off was unheard of. The wedding was held on the first Sabbath after Tishe b'Av, and included all that is customary at the marriage of a virgin: the banquet for the poor, the canopy before the synagogue, the musicians, the wedding jester, the virtue dance. Only one thing was lacking: joy. The bridegroom stood beneath the marriage canopy, a figure of desolation. The bride had recovered from her sickness, but had remained pale and thin. Her tears fell into the golden chicken broth. From all eyes the same question looked out: why had Anshel done it?

After Avigdor's marriage to Hadass, Peshe spread that rumor that Anshel had sold his wife to Avigdor for a price, and that the money had been supplied by Alter Vishkower. One young man pondered the riddle at great length until he finally arrived at the conclusion that Anshel had lost his beloved wife to Avigdor at cards, or even on a spin of the Hanukkah dreidl. It is a general rule that when the grain of truth cannot be found, men will swallow great helpings of falsehood. Truth itself is often concealed in such a way that the harder you look for it, the harder it is to find.

Not long after the wedding, Hadass became pregnant. The child was a boy and those assembled at the circumcision could scarcely believe their ears when they heard the father name his son Anshel.

The Cafeteria

I

Even though I have reached the point where a great part of my earnings is given away in taxes, I still have the habit of eating in cafeterias when I am by myself. I like to take a tray with a tin knife, fork, spoon, and paper napkin and to choose at the counter the food I enjoy. Besides, I meet there the *landsleit* from Poland, as well as all kinds of literary beginners and readers who know Yiddish. The moment I sit down at a table, they come over. 'Hello, Aaron!' they greet me, and we talk about Yiddish literature, the Holocaust, the state of Israel, and often about acquaintances who were eating rice pudding or stewed prunes the last time I was here and are already in their graves. Since I seldom read a paper, I learn this news only later. Each time, I am startled, but at my age one has to be ready for such tidings. The food sticks in the throat; we look at one another in confusion,

59

and our eyes ask mutely, Whose turn is next? Soon we begin to chew again. I am often reminded of a scene in a film about Africa. A lion attacks a herd of zebras and kills one. The frightened zebras run for a while and then they stop and start to graze again. Do they have a choice?

I cannot spend too long with these Yiddishists, because I am always busy. I am writing a novel, a story, an article. I have to lecture today or tomorrow; my datebook is crowded with all kinds of appointments for weeks and months in advance. It can happen that an hour after I leave the cafeteria I am on a train to Chicago or flying to California. But meanwhile we converse in the mother language and I hear of intrigues and pettiness about which, from a moral point of view, it would be better not to be informed. Everyone tries in his own way with all his means to grab as many honors and as much money and prestige as he can. None of us learns from all these deaths. Old age does not cleanse us. We don't repent at the gate of hell.

I have been moving around in this neighborhood for over thirty years – as long as I lived in Poland. I know each block, each house. There has been little building here on uptown Broadway in the last decades, and I have the illusion of having put down roots here. I have spoken in most of the synagogues. They know me in some of the stores and in the vegetarian restaurants. Women with whom I have had affairs live on the side streets. Even the pigeons know me; the moment I come out with a bag of feed, they begin to fly toward me from blocks away. It is an area that stretches from Ninety-sixth Street to Seventy-second Street and from Central Park to Riverside Drive. Almost every day on my walk after lunch, I pass the funeral parlor that waits for us and all our ambitions and illusions. Sometimes I imagine that the funeral parlor is also a kind of cafeteria where one gets a quick eulogy or Kaddish on the way to eternity.

The cafeteria people I meet are mostly men: old bachelors like myself, would-be writers, retired teachers, some with dubious doctorate titles, a rabbi without a congregation, a painter of Jewish themes, a few translators – all immigrants from Poland or Russia. I seldom know their names. One of them disappears and I think he is already in the next world; suddenly he reappears and he tells me that he has tried to settle in Tel Aviv or Los Angeles. Again he eats his rice pudding, sweetens his coffee with saccharin. He has a few more wrinkles, but he tells the same stories and makes the same gestures. It may happen that he takes a paper from his pocket and reads me a poem he has written.

*

It was in the fifties that a woman appeared in the group who looked younger than the rest of us. She must have been in her early thirties; she was short, slim, with a girlish face, brown hair that she wore in a bun, a short nose, and dimples in her cheeks. Her eyes were hazel – actually, of an indefinite color. She dressed in a modest European way. She spoke Polish, Russian, and an idiomatic Yiddish. She always carried Yiddish newspapers and magazines. She had been in a prison camp in Russia and had spent some time in the camps in Germany before she obtained a visa for the United States. The men all hovered around her. They didn't let her pay the check. They gallantly brought her coffee and cheesecake. They listened to her talk and jokes. She had returned from the devastation still gay. She was introduced to me. Her name was Esther. I didn't know if she was unmarried, a widow, a divorcée. She told me she was working in a factory, where she sorted buttons. This fresh young woman did not fit into the group of elderly has-beens. It was also hard to understand why she couldn't find a better job than sorting buttons in New Jersey. But I didn't ask too many questions. She told me that she had read my writing while still in Poland, and later in the camps in Germany after the war. She said to me, 'You are my writer.'

The moment she uttered those words I imagined

I was in love with her. We were sitting alone (the other man at our table had gone to make a telephone call), and I said, 'For such words I must kiss you.'

'Well, what are you waiting for?'

She gave me both a kiss and a bite.

I said, 'You are a ball of fire.'

'Yes, fire from Gehenna.'

A few days later, she invited me to her home. She lived on a street between Broadway and Riverside Drive with her father, who had no legs and sat in a wheelchair. His legs had been frozen in Siberia. He had tried to run away from one of Stalin's slave camps in the winter of 1944. He looked like a strong man, had a head of thick white hair, a ruddy face, and eyes full of energy. He spoke in a swaggering fashion, with boyish boastfulness and a cheerful laugh. In an hour, he told me his story. He was born in White Russia but he had lived long years in Warsaw, Lodz, and Vilna. In the beginning of the thirties, he became a Communist and soon afterward a functionary in the Party. In 1939 he escaped to Russia with his daughter. His wife and the other children remained in Nazi-occupied Warsaw. In Russia, somebody denounced him as a Trotskyite and he was sent to mine gold in the north. The G.P.U. sent people there to die. Even the strongest could not survive the cold and hunger for more than a year. They were exiled without a sentence. They died together: Zionists, Bundists, members of the Polish Socialist Party, Ukrainian Nationalists, and just refugees, all caught because of the labor shortage. They often died of scurvy or beriberi. Boris Merkin, Esther's father, spoke about this as if it were a big joke. He called the Stalinists outcasts, bandits, sycophants. He assured me that had it not been for the United States Hitler would have overrun all of Russia. He told how prisoners tricked the guards to get an extra piece of bread or a double portion of watery soup, and what methods were used in picking lice.

Esther called out, 'Father, enough!'

'What's the matter – am I lying?'

'One can have enough even of kreplaech.'

'Daughter, you did it yourself.'

When Esther went to the kitchen to make tea, I learned from her father that she had had a husband in Russia – a Polish Jew who had volunteered in the Red Army and perished in the war. Here in New York she was courted by a refugee, a former smuggler in Germany who had opened a bookbinding factory and become rich. 'Persuade her to marry him,' Boris Merkin said to me. 'It would be good for me, too.'

'Maybe she doesn't love him.'

'There is no such thing as love. Give me a cigarette. In the camp, people climbed on one another like worms.'

II

I had invited Esther to supper, but she called to say she had the grippe and must remain in bed. Then in a few days' time a situation arose that made me leave for Israel. On the way back, I stopped over in London and Paris. I wanted to write to Esther, but I had lost her address. When I returned to New York, I tried to call her, but there was no telephone listing for Boris Merkin or Esther Merkin – father and daughter must have been boarders in somebody else's apartment. Weeks passed and she did not show up in the cafeteria. I asked the group about her; nobody knew where she was. 'She has most probably married that bookbinder,' I said to myself. One evening, I went to the cafeteria with the premonition that I would find Esther there. I saw a black wall and boarded windows – the cafeteria had burned. The old bachelors were no doubt meeting in another cafeteria, or an Automat. But where? To search is not in my nature. I had plenty of complications without Esther.

The summer passed; it was winter. Late one day, I walked by the cafeteria and again saw lights, a counter, guests. The owners had rebuilt. I entered, took a check, and saw Esther sitting alone at a table reading a Yiddish newspaper. She did not notice me, and I observed her for a while. She wore a man's fur fez and a jacket trimmed with a faded fur collar. She looked pale, as though recuperating from a sickness. Could that grippe have been the start of a serious illness? I went over to her table and asked, 'What's new in buttons?'

She started and smiled. Then she called out, 'Miracles do happen!'

'Where have you been?'

'Where did you disappear to?' she replied. 'I thought you were still abroad.'

'Where are our cafeterianiks?'

'They now go to the cafeteria on Fifty-seventh Street and Eighth Avenue. They only reopened this place yesterday.'

'May I bring you a cup of coffee?'

'I drink too much coffee. All right.'

I went to get her coffee and a large egg cookie. While I stood at the counter, I turned my head and looked at her. Esther had taken off her mannish fur hat and smoothed her hair. She folded the newspaper, which meant that she was ready to talk. She got up and tilted the other chair against the table as a sign that the seat was taken. When I sat down, Esther said, 'You left without saying goodbye, and there I was about to knock at the pearly gates of heaven.'

'What happened?'

'Oh, the grippe became pneumonia. They gave me penicillin, and I am one of those who cannot take it. I got a rash all over my body. My father, too, is not well.'

'What's the matter with your father?'

'High blood pressure. He had a kind of stroke and his mouth became all crooked.'

'Oh, I'm sorry. Do you still work with buttons?'

'Yes, with buttons. At least I don't have to use my head, only my hands. I can think my own thoughts.'

'What do you think about?'

'What not. The other workers are all Puerto Ricans. They rattle away in Spanish from morning to night.'

'Who takes care of your father?'

'Who? Nobody. I come home in the evening to make supper. He has one desire – to marry me off for my own good and, perhaps, for his comfort, but I can't marry a man I don't love.'

'What is love?'

'You ask me! You write novels about it. But you're a man – I assume you really don't know what it is. A woman is a piece of merchandise to you. To me a man who talks nonsense or smiles like an idiot is repulsive. I would rather die than live with him. And a man who goes from one woman to another is not for me. I don't want to share with anybody.'

'I'm afraid a time is coming when everybody will.'

'That is not for me.'

'What kind of person was your husband?'

'How did you know I had a husband? My father, I suppose. The minute I leave the room, he prattles. My husband believed in things and was ready to die for them. He was not exactly my type but I respected him and loved him, too. He wanted to die and he died like a hero. What else can I say?'

'And the others?'

'There were no others. Men were after me. The way people behaved in the war – you will never know. They lost all shame. On the bunks near me one time, a mother lay with one man and her daughter with another. People were like beasts – worse than beasts. In the middle of it all, I dreamed about love. Now I have even stopped dreaming. The men who come here are terrible bores. Most of them are half mad, too. One of them tried to read me a forty-page poem. I almost fainted.'

'I wouldn't read you anything I'd written.'

'I've been told how you behave – no!'

'No is no. Drink your coffee.'

'You don't even try to persuade me. Most men around here plague you and you can't get rid of them. In Russia people suffered, but I have never met as many maniacs there as in New York City. The building where

I live is a madhouse. My neighbors are lunatics. They accuse each other of all kinds of things. They sing, cry, break dishes. One of them jumped out of the window and killed herself. She was having an affair with a boy twenty years younger. In Russia the problem was to escape the lice; here you're surrounded by insanity.'

We drank coffee and shared the egg cookie. Esther put down her cup. 'I can't believe that I'm sitting with you at this table. I read all your articles under all your pen names. You tell so much about yourself I have the feeling I've known you for years. Still, you are a riddle to me.'

'Men and women can never understand one another.'

'No – I cannot understand my own father. Sometimes he is a complete stranger to me. He won't live long.'

'Is he so sick?'

'It's everything together. He's lost the will to live. Why live without legs, without friends, without a family? They have all perished. He sits and reads the newspapers all day long. He acts as though he were interested in what's going on in the world. His ideals are gone, but he still hopes for a just revolution. How can a revolution help him? I myself never put my hopes in any movement or party. How can we hope when everything ends in death?'

'Hope in itself is a proof that there is no death.'

'Yes, I know you often write about this. For me, death is the only comfort. What do the dead do? They continue to drink coffee and eat egg cookies? They still read newspapers? A life after death would be nothing but a joke.'

III

Some of the cafeterianiks came back to the rebuilt cafeteria. New people appeared – all of them Europeans. They launched into long discussions in Yiddish, Polish, Russian, even Hebrew. Some of those who came from Hungary mixed German, Hungarian, Yiddish-German – then all of a sudden they began to speak plain Galician Yiddish. They asked to have their coffee in glasses, and held lumps of sugar between their teeth when they drank. Many of them were my readers. They introduced themselves and reproached me for all kinds of literary errors: I contradicted myself, went too far in descriptions of sex, described Jews in such a way that anti-Semites could use it for propaganda. They told me their experiences in the ghettos, in the Nazi concentration camps, in Russia. They pointed out one another. 'Do you see that fellow – in Russia he immediately became a Stalinist. He denounced his own friends. Here in America he has switched to anti-Bolshevism.' The one who was spoken about seemed to sense that he was being maligned, because the moment my informant left he took his cup of coffee and his rice pudding, sat down at my table, and said, 'Don't believe a word of what you are told. They invent all kinds of lies. What could you do in a country where the rope was always around your neck? You had to adjust yourself if you wanted to live and not die somewhere in Kazakhstan. To get a bowl of soup or a place to stay you had to sell your soul.'

There was a table with a group of refugees who ignored me. They were not interested in literature and journalism but strictly in business. In Germany they had been smugglers. They seemed to be doing shady business here, too; they whispered to one another and winked, counted their money, wrote long lists of numbers. Somebody pointed out one of them. 'He had a store in Auschwitz.'

'What do you mean, a store?'

'God help us. He kept his merchandise in the straw where he slept – a rotten potato, sometimes a piece of soap, a tin spoon, a little fat. Still, he did business. Later, in Germany, he became such a big smuggler they once took forty thousand dollars away from him.'

Isaac Bashevis Singer

Sometimes months passed between my visits to the
cafeteria. A year or two had gone by (perhaps three or
four; I lost count), and Esther did not show up. I asked
about her a few times. Someone said that she was going
to the cafeteria on Forty-second Street; another had
heard that she was married. I learned that some of the
cafeterianiks had died. They were beginning to settle
down in the United States, had remarried, opened busi-
nesses, workshops, even had children again. Then came
cancer or a heart attack. The result of the Hitler and
Stalin years, it was said.

One day, I entered the cafeteria and saw Esther. She
was sitting alone at a table. It was the same Esther. She
was even wearing the same fur hat, but a strand of gray
hair fell over her forehead. How strange – the fur hat,
too, seemed to have grayed. The other cafeterianiks did
not appear to be interested in her any more, or they did
not know her. Her face told of the time that had passed.
There were shadows under her eyes. Her gaze was no
longer so clear. Around her mouth was an expression
that could be called bitterness, disenchantment. I greeted
her. She smiled, but her smile immediately faded away.
I asked, 'What happened to you?'

'Oh, I'm still alive.'

'May I sit down?'

'Please – certainly.'

72

'May I bring you a cup of coffee?'

'No. Well, if you insist.'

I noticed that she was smoking, and also that she was reading not the newspaper to which I contribute but a competition paper. She had gone over to the enemy. I brought her coffee and for myself stewed prunes – a remedy for constipation. I sat down. 'Where were you all this time? I have asked for you.'

'Really? Thank you.'

'What happened?'

'Nothing good.' She looked at me. I knew that she saw in me what I saw in her: the slow wilting of the flesh. She said, 'You have no hair but you are white.'

For a while we were silent. Then I said, 'Your father –' and as I said it I knew that her father was not alive.

Esther said, 'He has been dead for almost a year.'

'Do you still sort buttons?'

'No, I became an operator in a dress shop.'

'What happened to you personally, may I ask?'

'Oh nothing – absolutely nothing. You will not believe it, but I was sitting here thinking about you. I have fallen into some kind of trap. I don't know what to call it. I thought perhaps you could advise me. Do you still have the patience to listen to the troubles of little people like me? No, I didn't mean to insult you. I even doubted you would remember me. To make it short,

73

I work but work is growing more difficult for me. I suffer from arthritis. I feel as if my bones would crack. I wake up in the morning and can't sit up. One doctor tells me that it's a disc in my back, others try to cure my nerves. One took X-rays and says that I have a tumor. He wanted me to go to the hospital for a few weeks, but I'm in no hurry for an operation. Suddenly a little lawyer showed up. He is a refugee himself and is connected with the German government. You know they're now giving reparation money. It's true that I escaped to Russia, but I'm a victim of the Nazis just the same. Besides, they don't know my biography so exactly. I could get a pension plus a few thousand dollars, but my dislocated disc is no good for the purpose because I got it later – after the camps. This lawyer says my only chance is to convince them that I am ruined psychically. It's the bitter truth, but how can you prove it? The German doctors, the neurologists, the psychiatrists require proof. Everything has to be according to the textbooks – just so and no different. The lawyer wants me to play insane. Naturally, he gets twenty percent of the reparation money – maybe more. Why he needs so much money I don't understand. He's already in his seventies, an old bachelor. He tried to make love to me and whatnot. He's half meshugga himself. But how can I play insane when actually I *am* insane? The whole thing revolts me and I'm afraid it will really drive me crazy. I hate swindle. But this shyster pursues me. I don't sleep. When the alarm rings in the morning, I wake up as shattered as I used to be in Russia when I had to walk to the forest and saw logs at four in the morning. Naturally, I take sleeping pills – if I didn't, I couldn't sleep at all. That is more or less the situation.'

'Why don't you get married? You are still a good-looking woman.'

'Well, the old question – there is nobody. It's too late. If you knew how I felt, you wouldn't ask such a question.'

IV

A few weeks passed. Snow had been falling. After the snow came rain, then frost. I stood at my window and looked out at Broadway. The passers-by half walked, half slipped. Cars moved slowly. The sky above the roofs shone violet, without a moon, without stars, and even though it was eight o'clock in the evening the light and the emptiness reminded me of dawn. The stores were deserted. For a moment, I had the feeling I was in Warsaw. The telephone rang and I rushed to answer it as I did ten, twenty, thirty years ago – still expecting the good tidings that a telephone call was about to bring me. I said hello, but there was no answer and I was seized by the fear that some evil power was trying to keep back the good news at the last minute. Then I heard a stammering. A woman's voice muttered my name.

'Yes, it is I.'

'Excuse me for disturbing you. My name is Esther. We met a few weeks ago in the cafeteria – '

'Esther!' I exclaimed.

'I don't know how I got the courage to phone you. I need to talk to you about something. Naturally, if you have the time and – please forgive my presumption.'

'No presumption. Would you like to come to my apartment?'

'If I will not be interrupting. It's difficult to talk in the cafeteria. It's noisy and there are eavesdroppers. What I want to tell you is a secret I wouldn't trust to anyone else.'

'Please, come up.'

I gave Esther directions. Then I tried to make order in my apartment, but I soon realized this was impossible. Letters, manuscripts lay around on tables and chairs. In the corners books and magazines were piled high. I opened the closets and threw inside whatever was under my hand: jackets, pants, shirts, shoes, slippers.

I picked up an envelope and to my amazement saw that it had never been opened. I tore it open and found a check. 'What's the matter with me – have I lost my mind?' I said out loud. I tried to read the letter that came with the check, but I had misplaced my glasses; my fountain pen was gone, too. Well – and where were my keys? I heard a bell ring and I didn't know whether it was the door or the telephone. I opened the door and saw Esther. It must have been snowing again, because her hat and the shoulders of her coat were trimmed with white. I asked her in, and my neighbor, the divorcée, who spied on me openly with no shame – and, God knows, with no sense of purpose – opened her door and stared at my guest.

Esther removed her boots and I took her coat and put it on the case of the *Encyclopaedia Britannica*. I shoved a few manuscripts off the sofa so she could sit down. I said, 'In my house there is sheer chaos.'

'It doesn't matter.'

I sat in an armchair strewn with socks and handkerchiefs. For a while we spoke about the weather, about the danger of being out in New York at night – even early in the evening. Then Esther said, 'Do you remember the time I spoke to you about my lawyer – that I had to go to a psychiatrist because of the reparation money?'

'Yes, I remember.'

'I didn't tell you everything. It was too wild. It still seems unbelievable, even to me. Don't interrupt me, I implore you. I'm not completely healthy – I may even say that I'm sick – but I know the difference between fact and illusion. I haven't slept for nights, and I kept wondering whether I should call you or not. I decided not to – but this evening it occurred to me that if I couldn't trust you with a thing like this, then there is no one I could talk to. I read you and I know that you have a sense of the great mysteries –' Esther said all this stammering and with pauses. For a moment her eyes smiled, and then they became sad and wavering.

I said, 'You can tell me everything.'

'I am afraid that you'll think me insane.'

'I swear I will not.'

Esther bit her lower lip. 'I want you to know that I saw Hitler,' she said.

Even though I was prepared for something unusual, my throat constricted. 'When – where?'

'You see, you are frightened already. It happened three years ago – almost four. I saw him here on Broadway.'

'On the street?'

'In the cafeteria.'

I tried to swallow the lump in my throat. 'Most probably someone resembling him,' I said finally.

'I knew you would say that. But remember, you've promised to listen. You recall the fire in the cafeteria?'

'Yes, certainly.'

'The fire has to do with it. Since you don't believe me anyhow, why draw it out? It happened this way. That night I didn't sleep. Usually when I can't sleep, I get up and make tea, or I try to read a book, but this time some power commanded me to get dressed and go out. I can't explain to you how I dared walk on Broadway at that late hour. It must have been two or three o'clock. I reached the cafeteria, thinking perhaps it stays open all night. I tried to look in, but the large window was covered by a curtain. There was a pale glow inside. I tried the revolving door and it turned. I went in and saw a scene I will not forget to the last day of my life. The tables were shoved together and around them sat men in white robes, like doctors or orderlies, all with swastikas on their sleeves. At the head sat Hitler. I beg you to hear me out – even a deranged person sometimes deserves to be listened to. They all spoke German. They didn't see me. They were busy with the Führer. It grew quiet and he started to talk. That abominable voice – I heard it many times on the radio. I didn't make out exactly what he said. I was too terrified to take it in. Suddenly one of his henchmen looked back at me and jumped up from his chair. How I came out alive I will never know. I ran with all my strength, and I was trembling all over. When I got home, I said to myself, "Esther, you are not right in the head." I still don't know how I lived through that night. The next morning, I didn't go straight to work but walked to the cafeteria to see if it was really there. Such an experience makes a person doubt his own senses. When I arrived, I found the place had burned down. When I saw this, I knew it had to do with what I had seen. Those who were there wanted all traces erased. These are the plain facts. I have no reason to fabricate such queer things.'

We were both silent. Then I said, 'You had a vision.'

'What do you mean, a vision?'

'The past is not lost. An image from years ago remained present somewhere in the fourth dimension and it reached you just at that moment.'

'As far as I know, Hitler never wore a long white robe.'

'Perhaps he did.'

'Why did the cafeteria burn down just that night?' Esther asked.

'It could be that the fire evoked the vision.'

'There was no fire then. Somehow I foresaw that you would give me this kind of explanation. If this was a vision, my sitting here with you is also a vision.'

'It couldn't have been anything else. Even if Hitler is

living and is hiding out in the United States, he is not likely to meet his cronies at a cafeteria on Broadway. Besides, the cafeteria belongs to a Jew.'

'I saw him as I am seeing you now.'

'You had a glimpse back in time.'

'Well, let it be so. But since then I have had no rest. I keep thinking about it. If I am destined to lose my mind, this will drive me to it.'

The telephone rang and I jumped up with a start. It was a wrong number. I sat down again. 'What about the psychiatrist your lawyer sent you to? Tell it to him and you'll get full compensation.'

Esther looked at me sidewise and unfriendly. 'I know what you mean. I haven't fallen that low yet.'

V

I was afraid that Esther would continue to call me. I even planned to change my telephone number. But weeks and months passed and I never heard from her or saw her. I didn't go to the cafeteria. But I often thought about her. How can the brain produce such nightmares? What goes on in that little marrow behind the skull? And what guarantee do I have that the same sort of thing will not happen to me? And how do we know that the human species will not end like this? I have played with the idea that all of humanity suffers from schizophrenia. Along with the atom, the personality of *Homo sapiens* has been splitting. When it comes to technology, the brain still functions, but in everything else degeneration has begun. They are all insane: the Communists, the Fascists, the preachers of democracy, the writers, the painters, the clergy, the atheists. Soon technology, too, will disintegrate. Buildings will collapse, power plants will stop generating electricity. Generals will drop atomic bombs on their own populations. Mad revolutionaries will run in the streets, crying fantastic slogans. I have often thought that it would begin in New York. This metropolis has all the symptoms of a mind gone berserk.

But since insanity has not yet taken over altogether, one has to act as though there were still order – according to Vaihinger's principle of 'as if.' I continued with my scribbling. I delivered manuscripts to the publisher. I lectured. Four times a year, I sent checks to the federal government, the state. What was left after my expenses I put in the savings bank. A teller entered some numbers in my bankbook and this meant that I was provided for. Somebody printed a few lines in a magazine or newspaper, and this signified that my value as a writer had gone up. I saw with amazement that all my efforts turned into paper. My apartment was one big waste-paper basket. From day to day, all this paper was getting drier and more parched. I woke up at night fearful that it would ignite. There was not an hour when I did not hear the sirens of fire engines.

A year after I had last seen Esther, I was going to Toronto to read a paper about Yiddish in the second half of the nineteenth century. I put a few shirts in my valise as well as papers of all kinds, among them one that made me a citizen of the United States. I had enough paper money in my pocket to pay for a taxi to Grand Central. But the taxis seemed to be taken. Those that were not refused to stop. Didn't the drivers see me? Had I suddenly become one of those who see and are not seen? I decided to take the subway. On my way, I saw Esther. She was not alone but with someone I had known years ago, soon after I arrived in the United States. He was a frequenter of a cafeteria on East Broadway. He used to sit at a table, express opinions, criticize, grumble. He was a small man, with sunken cheeks the color of brick, and bulging eyes. He was angry at the new writers. He belittled the old ones. He rolled his own cigarettes and dropped ashes into the plates from which we ate. Almost two decades had passed since I had last seen him. Suddenly he appears with Esther. He was even holding her arm. I had never seen Esther look so well. She was wearing a new coat, a new hat. She smiled at me and nodded. I wanted to stop her, but my watch showed that it was late. I barely managed to catch the train. In my bedroom, the bed was already made. I undressed and went to sleep.

In the middle of the night, I awoke. My car was being switched, and I almost fell out of bed. I could not sleep any more and I tried to remember the name of the little man I had seen with Esther. But I was unable to. The thing I did remember was that even thirty years ago he had been far from young. He had come to the United States in 1905 after the revolution in Russia. In Europe, he had a reputation as a speaker and public figure. How old must he be now? According to my calculations, he had to be in the late eighties – perhaps even ninety. Is it possible that Esther could be intimate with such an old man? But this evening he had not looked old. The longer I brooded about it in the darkness, the stranger the encounter seemed to me. I even imagined that somewhere in a newspaper I had read that he had died. Do corpses walk around on Broadway? This would mean that Esther, too, was not living. I raised the window shade and sat up and looked out into the night – black, impenetrable, without a moon. A few stars ran along with the train for a while and then they disappeared. A lighted factory emerged; I saw machines but no operators. Then it was swallowed in the darkness and another group of stars began to follow the train. I was turning with the earth on its axis. I was circling with it around the sun and moving in the direction of a constellation whose name I had forgotten. Is there no death? Or is there no life?

I thought about what Esther had told me of seeing Hitler in the cafeteria. It had seemed utter nonsense, but now I began to reappraise the idea. If time and space are nothing more than forms of perception, as Kant argues, and quality, quantity, causality are only categories of thinking, why shouldn't Hitler confer with his Nazis in a cafeteria on Broadway? Esther didn't sound insane. She had seen a piece of reality that the heavenly censorship prohibits as a rule. She had caught a glimpse behind the curtain of the phenomena. I regretted that I had not asked for more details.

In Toronto, I had little time to ponder these matters, but when I returned to New York I went to the cafeteria for some private investigation. I met only one man I knew: a rabbi who had become an agnostic and given up his job. I asked him about Esther. He said, 'The pretty little woman who used to come here?'

'Yes.'

'I heard that she committed suicide.'

'When – how?'

'I don't know. Perhaps we are not speaking about the same person.'

No matter how many questions I asked and how much I described Esther, everything remained vague. Some young woman who used to come here had turned on the gas and made an end of herself – that was all the ex-rabbi could tell me.

I decided not to rest until I knew for certain what had happened to Esther and also to that half writer, half politician I remembered from East Broadway. But I grew busier from day to day. The cafeteria closed. The neighborhood changed. Years have passed and I have never seen Esther again. Yes, corpses do walk on Broadway. But why did Esther choose that particular corpse? She could have got a better bargain even in this world.

a little history

Penguin Modern Classics were launched in 1961, and have been shaping the reading habits of generations ever since.

The list began with distinctive grey spines and evocative pictorial covers – a look that, after various incarnations, continues to influence their current design – and with books that are still considered landmark classics today.

Penguin Modern Classics have caused scandal and political change, inspired great films and broken down barriers, whether social, sexual or the boundaries of language itself. They remain the most provocative, groundbreaking, exciting and revolutionary works of the last 100 years (or so).

In 2011, on the fiftieth anniversary of the Modern Classics, we're publishing fifty Mini Modern Classics: the very best short fiction by writers ranging from Beckett to Conrad, Nabokov to Saki, Updike to Wodehouse. Though they don't take long to read, they'll stay with you long after you turn the final page.

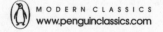
MODERN CLASSICS
www.penguinclassics.com